How I Found a Friend

HOW I FOUND A FRIEND

Irina Hale

SCHOLASTIC INC.
New York Toronto London Auckland Sydney

 Published by Scholastic Inc., 730 Broadway, New York, NY 10003, by arrangement with Viking Penguin, a division of Penguin Books USA Inc.
Printed in the U.S.A.
Set in 24 point Horley Old Style Semi.
ISBN 0-590-46969-X
ISBN 0-590-29046-0 (meets NASTA specifications)

4 5 6 7 8 9 10 09 00 99 98 97 96 95 94

For Julie

One day a strange boy walked past my house.
"What a fine bear he has," I thought.
"And what a very nice baseball cap.
I wish that boy was my friend."

When the boy came past again,
I was holding my bear.
And I had put on
my cowboy hat.

The next day I put my bear
up on the wall.

When the boy came, he wanted to take my bear and leave his bear in its place. "I like trading things," he said.

But his mother told him to
leave other people's bears alone.

The next day my bear was
wearing my cowboy hat.

And the other boy's bear
was wearing his baseball cap.

“Hello!” says the boy’s bear to my bear.

“I like your hat.”

“Hello!” says my bear. “I like your hat, too. Will you be my friend?”

"Yes," says the boy's bear. "And let's change hats. I like trading things."

When night came, the two bears
sat together in the moonlight.

I was surprised the next morning when I found that the bears had exchanged hats.

The other boy was surprised, too.

"I wonder how it happened?"
he asked me.

"Would you like to
come in and have tea?"
said my mother to his mother.

While our mothers drank tea, the boy and I watched TV and ate popcorn.

Our bears watched with us.

We are friends.